JANE YOLEN & MARK

How Do Dinosaurs Play All Day?

SCHOLASTIC INC.

New York   Toronto   London   Auckland
Sydney   Mexico City   New Delhi   Hong Kong

Dinosaur days—are they happy or icky?
Dinosaur ways are so often quite tricky.

Do dinosaurs slump?

Do they grump?

Do they groan?

Do they lie
on top of
their covers
and moan?

No . . .
please *stick* around,
very soon you will find
that dinosaur days
are the very best kind.

NEOVENATOR

Does a dinosaur sit
at the table and pout?

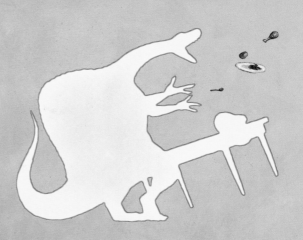

Does she throw
her breakfast plate
all about?

Does she spill out her milk

or play with her eggs?

Does she let the juice run down
all over her legs?

No . . .
she eats each bite
and is always polite.

PACHYCEPHALOSAURUS

Does a dinosaur grumble
each time he is ill?

Does he kick at
the tissues?
Spit out
every
pill?

No . . .
a dinosaur
reads

every
sweet
get-well
card.

He drinks all
his cocoa—
it's not
very hard.

STYRACOSAURUS

Bed rest
is best.

PAGES 2-3

PAGES 4-5

PAGES 8-9

PAGES 10-11

PAGES 12-13

PAGES 14-15

PAGE 16

Does a dinosaur always
act like the class clown?
Does he handstand on tables
or hang upside down?

No . . .
he paints,

writes,

and reads
in his own
quiet way,

then raises
his hand
when there's
something
to say.

In order
to learn,
dinosaurs
take a turn.

How does a dinosaur
play well outside?

Does he push other kids
for a turn on the slide?

Does he hog all the blocks, the jump rope, and the ball,

not
letting
the others
enjoy things
at all?

10

No . . .
that's not fair.
Dinosaurs share.

SEGNOSAURUS

TYRANNOSAURUS REX

How does a dinosaur
get ready to nap?

Does she growl, does she grumble?
Does she spit, snarl, or snap?

Does she play with her train,

with her bubbles,   or ball?

Does she
never
lie down
in her
bedroom
at all?

No . . .
she sleeps a bit
and rises fit.

Are dinosaurs mean?
Do they often forget
that they have to take care
of each special pet?

No . . .
a dinosaur gives
his dear dog a
sweet treat.

Or he pets
his cute cat
from its head
to its feet.

He cuddles
his teddy.

He kisses his duckie.

SPINOSAURUS

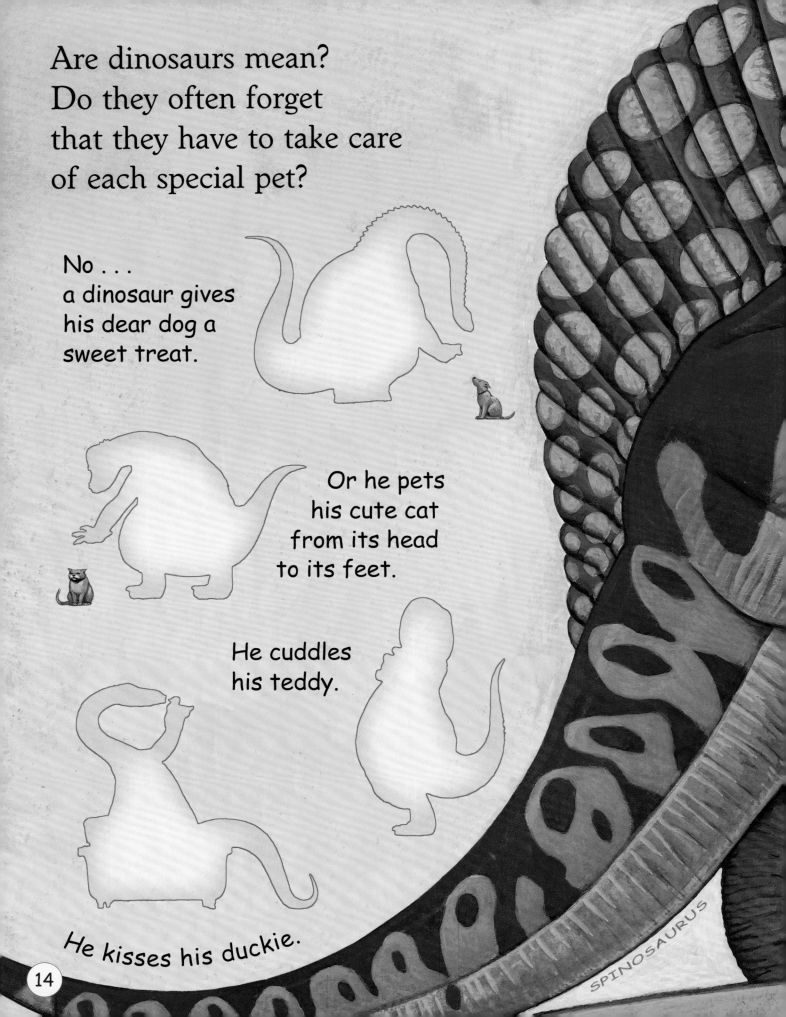

A dinosaur's pet
is really quite
lucky.

How does a dinosaur show her true love?
Does she bounce, does she pounce?
Does she push,
does she shove?

No . . .
a dinosaur kisses,
makes hearts,
even bakes.

She gives hugs
and flowers,

and valentine
cakes.

ANTARCTOSAURUS

Love is
known
when it
is shown.

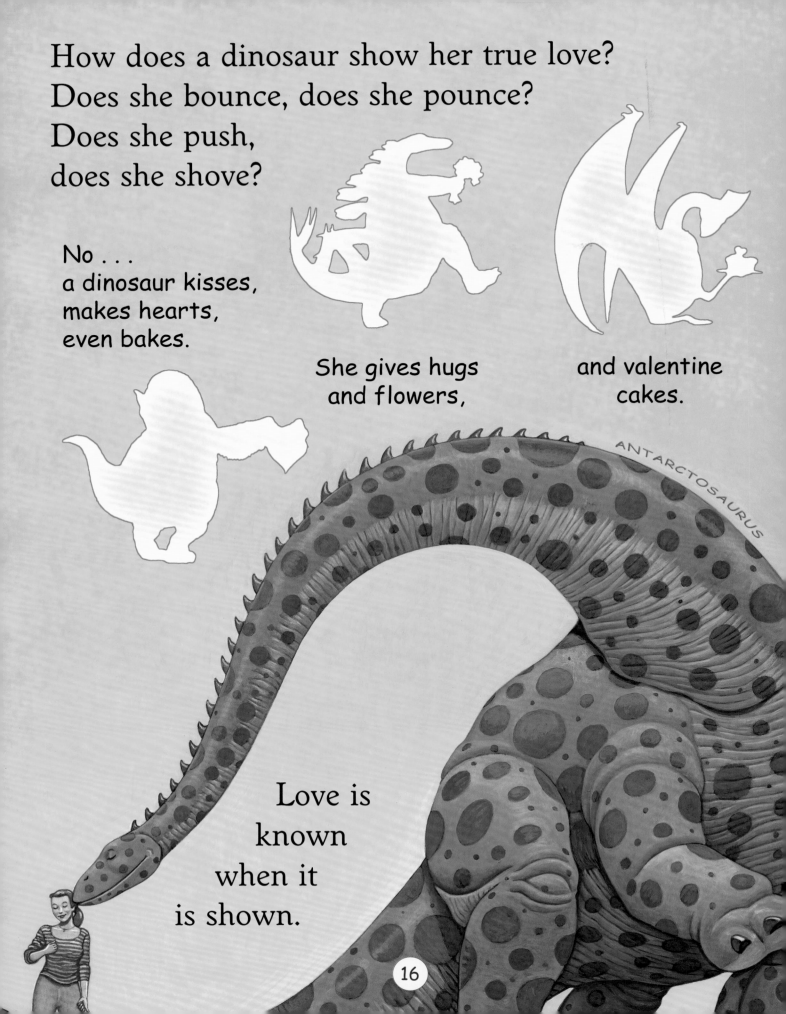